LITTLE TIGER PRESS
An imprint of Magi Publications
1 The Coda Centre, 189 Munster Road,
London SW6 6AW, UK
www.littletigerpress.com
This volume copyright © Magi Publications 2006
All rights reserved
ISBN-10: 1-84506-447-X
ISBN-13: 978-1-84506-447-1
Printed in China
2 4 6 8 10 9 7 5 3 1

Snuggle Up, Sleepy Ones
Claire Freedman
Illustrated by Tina Macnaughton
First published in Great Britain 2005
by Little Tiger Press,
an imprint of Magi Publications
Text copyright © Claire Freedman 2004
Illustrations copyright © Tina Macnaughton 2004

Can't you sleep, Dotty?
Tim Warnes
First published in Great Britain 2001
by Little Tiger Press,
an imprint of Magi Publications
Text and illustrations copyright
© Tim Warnes 2001

Little Bunny's Bathtime!
Jane Johnson
Illustrated by Gaby Hansen
First published in Great Britain 2004
by Little Tiger Press,
an imprint of Magi Publications
Text copyright © Jane Johnson 2004
Illustrations copyright © Gaby Hansen 2004

Quiet!
Paul Bright
Illustrated by Guy Parker-Rees
First published in Great Britain 2003
by Little Tiger Press,
an imprint of Magi Publications
Text copyright © Paul Bright 2003
Illustrations copyright © Guy Parker-Rees 2003

Time to Sleep, Alfie Bear!
Catherine Walters
First published in Great Britain 2003
by Little Tiger Press,
an imprint of Magi Publications
Text and illustrations copyright
© Catherine Walters 2003

Two Hungry Bears
Linda Cornwell
Illustrated by Jane Chapman
First published in Great Britain 2000
by Little Tiger Press,
an imprint of Magi Publications
Text copyright © Linda Cornwell 2000
Illustrations copyright © Jane Chapman 2000

Sweet Dreams, My Little One

A Treasury of Stories for Bedtime

Snuggle Up, Sleepy Ones

Claire Freedman   Tina Macnaughton

The sun paints the sky
a warm, glowing red.
It's time to stop playing,
it's time for bed.

In the soft swampy mud
baby hippo, so snug,
Cuddles up close
for a big hippo hug.

13

Through wild, waving grasses
shy antelope roam.

14

It's been a long day,
they're ready for home.

15

16

Bold leopard cubs rest
from practising roars.
They snuggle together,
all tired, tangled paws.

Whilst up in the treetops
birds twitter and cheep,

18

Till quieter and quieter,
they fall fast asleep.

Below in their nests
baby porcupines all
Curl up, so snug tight,
in one spiky ball.

With tired, drooping necks
giraffe flop to the ground.
Sheltered and watched over.
Safe and sound.

And mischievous monkeys
shout down from the trees,
"It's not really dark yet.
Five more minutes, please!"

24

Zebras lay panting,
tired out from their play.
They sink into sleep
as the sun slips away.

Moths come a-fluttering,
bats flitter by.
Elephants rumble
their deep lullaby.

29

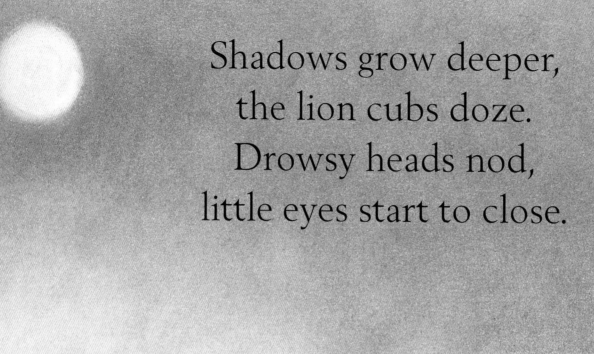

Shadows grow deeper,
the lion cubs doze.
Drowsy heads nod,
little eyes start to close.

Stars twinkle brightly,
the moon softly gleams.
Snuggle up, sleepy ones.
Hush now, sweet dreams!

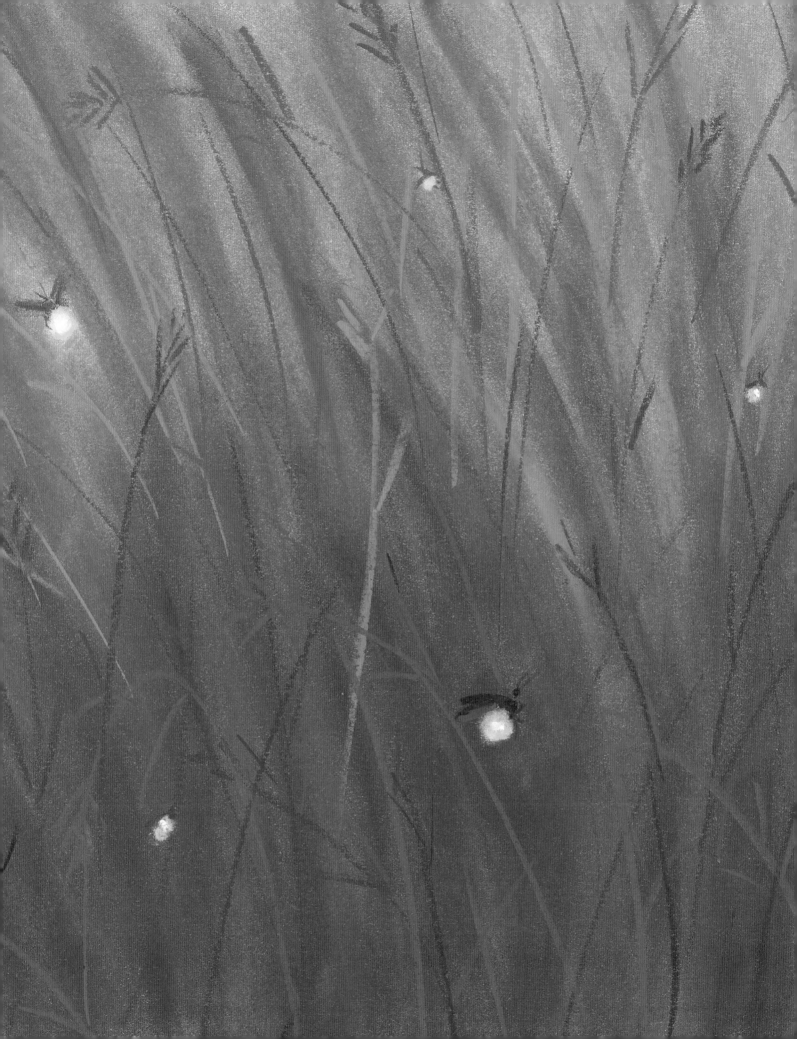

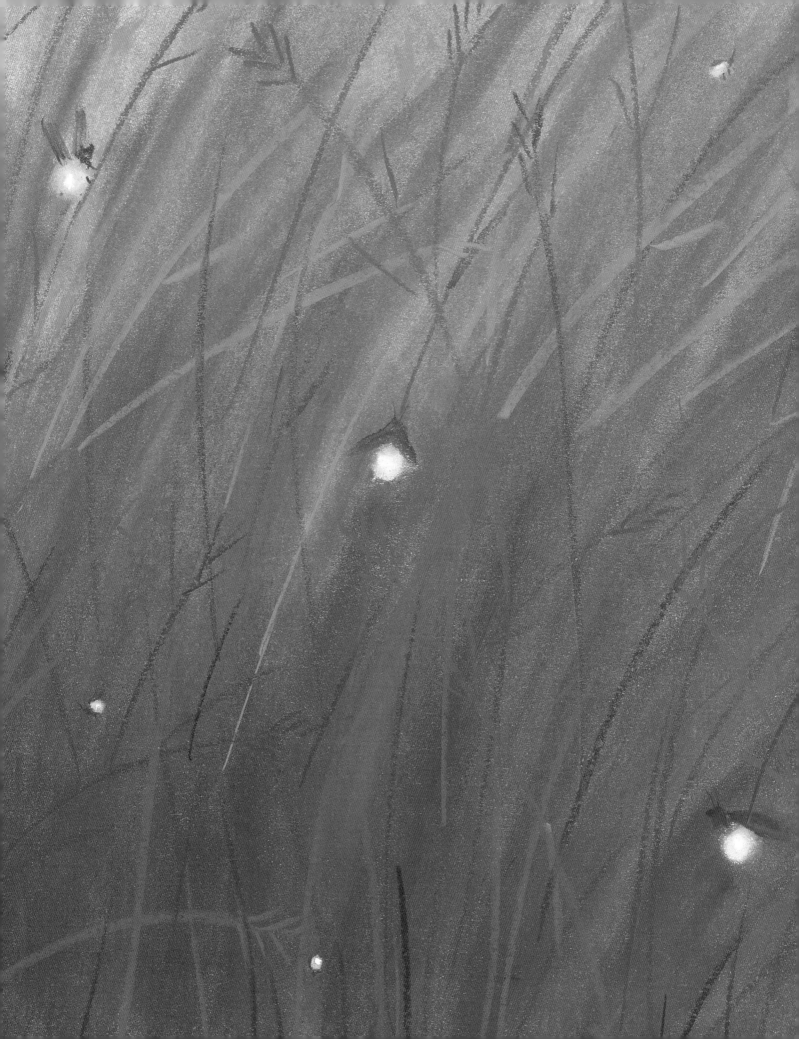

Can't you sleep, Dotty?

★ ★ ★

Tim Warnes

38

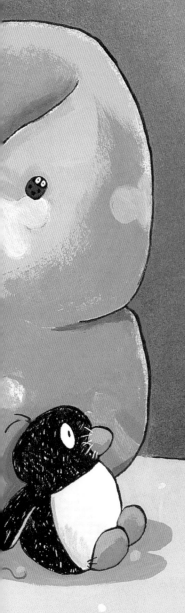

Dotty couldn't sleep.
It was her first night
in her new home.

She tried sleeping
upside down.

She tried
snuggling up
to Penguin.

She even tried
lying on the
floor.

AWOOOOOOOOOOOooo°

But still Dotty
couldn't sleep.

Dotty's howling woke up Pip the mouse. "Can't you sleep, Dotty?" he asked. "Perhaps you should try counting the stars like I do."

43

But Dotty could only count up to one. *That* wasn't enough to send her to sleep.

What could she do next?

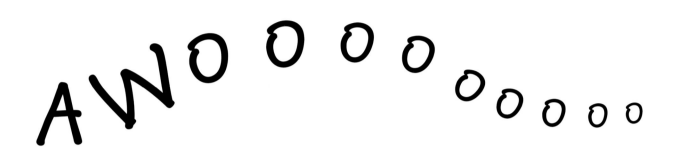

45

Susie the bird was awake now. "Can't you sleep, Dotty?" she twittered. "I always have a little drink before I go to bed."

Chirp!

Chirp!

Dotty went to her bowl and
had a little drink.

Slurp!
Slurp!

But then she made
a little puddle.
Well *that*
didn't help!
What *could* Dotty
do to get to sleep?

AWOOOOOOOOOO o o

Whiskers the rabbit had woken up, too.
"Can't you sleep, Dotty?" he mumbled
sleepily. "I hide away in my burrow
at bedtime. That always works."

Wag! Wag!

51

Dotty dived under her blanket so that only her bottom was showing. But it was all dark under there with no light at all.

Dotty was too scared to go to sleep.

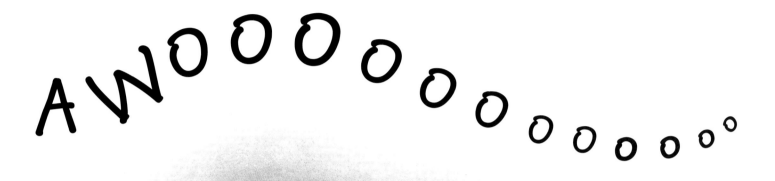

Flump!

53

Tommy the tortoise poked his head from out of his shell.

"Can't you sleep, Dotty?" he sighed. "I like to sleep where it's bright and sunny."

Plod
Plod

54

Dotty liked that idea . . .

and turned on her torch!

"Turn it off, Dotty!"
shouted all her friends.
"*We* can't get to sleep now!"

Poor Dotty was too
tired to try anything else.
Then Tommy had a great idea . . .

he helped Dotty into her bed.
What Dotty needed for the first
night in her new home was . . .

to snuggle up among
all her new friends. Soon
they were all fast asleep.
Night night, Dotty.
Sleep tight!

ZZZZZZZzz

Little Bunny's Bathtime!

Jane Johnson

illustrated by

Gaby Hansen

"Bathtime for my bunnies!"
called Mrs Rabbit, and her
children all came running.
All except her youngest
little bunny.

"I don't want a bath,"
said Little Bunny.
"I want to go on playing."

"You really want to play all by
yourself?" asked his mummy.
Little Bunny nodded, but
now he wasn't so sure.

"Well, you be good while
I'm busy with the others,"
said Mrs Rabbit, plopping
them into the water.

"Swish, swash, swoosh,"
sang the little rabbits happily,
swirling their bubbles into
a heap.

Little Bunny wanted
to play too.

"Look at me!" he called,
hiding behind the towels.

"Yes, dear," said Mrs Rabbit, but
she went on washing the others.
"Tickly, wickly, wiggle toes," giggled
her little bunnies, waggling their
feet in the water.

"Guess where I am!"
shouted Little Bunny,
hidden in the linen
basket.

"Found you," smiled his
mother, lifting the lid . . .

But she turned back
to finish washing
the others.

"Up you come!" puffed Mrs Rabbit,
lifting her children out of the tub.

"Rub-a-dub-dub, you've all had a scrub!"
she laughed. "What lovely clean
bunnies you are!"

Little Bunny was cross.
He wanted his mummy
to notice *him*.

So he
climbed
up . . .

and up – as far
as he could.
But suddenly . . .

· · · SPLOSH!

He fell into the bath!

"Oh my!" said Mrs Rabbit, fishing
him out straight away.

Little Bunny gazed up at her happily.
"I'm ready for a bath now, Mummy,"
he said, smiling sweetly.

Mrs Rabbit couldn't
help smiling back.
"Off you go and play
quietly," she said to
the others.

Then she ran
fresh water and gave
Little Bunny a bath —
all to himself.

83

"Soapy ears and soapy toes,
   soapy little bunny nose!" sang Mrs Rabbit.
   She washed his ears while he fluffed
up some new bubbles.
   "I love you, Mummy," said Little Bunny.
   "I love you too, darling."

She washed his back while
he played with his boat.
"You're my best mummy in the
whole world," said Little Bunny.
"And you're my precious
bunnykin."

She dried his fur
and whiskers, and said,
"Ooh, you smell
so clean and nice!"

And Little Bunny kissed his mummy
and hugged her tight.

"There now, all done," sighed Mrs Rabbit.
"It's time for bed. Where are my other
little bunnies?"

She found them in the kitchen.
"Oh no! What a mess!" cried
Mrs Rabbit. "You're dirty again!
You all need *another* bath!"

"Yes," giggled Little Bunny.
"All except me!"

Deep, deep in the jungle, chimps were chattering,
frogs were croaking,

birds were screeching, and a million insects
were humming and buzzing. What a lot of noise!

It was time for baby Leo to have his morning nap.
"He'll never get to sleep with all this din," said Ma Lion.
"Isn't there something you can do?"

"Do?" said Pa Lion. "Do? I am king of the beasts.
Of course there is something I can do!" He stood up tall,
puffed out his huge chest, and roared . . .

And baby Leo slept. Pa Lion whispered softly,
but so clearly that all of the creatures could hear him:
"And if any of you makes a noise, and wakes up Leo, I will eat you."

All was quiet in the jungle. Quiet as the morning mist.
Quiet as the opening flowers.
Quiet as a baby sleeping. Suddenly . . .

Cawing and crowing, squeaking and squawking.
Beaks pecking and claws scratching.
Two parrots were arguing
in the bushes!

"Quiet!" said Pa Lion, as loud as he dared.
"It's all right," said Ma Lion. "Leo's still fast asleep."
"I can't eat the parrots, then," said Pa Lion sulkily.
"No, my dear," said Ma Lion, "you can't eat the parrots."
"Bother," said Pa Lion. "I could do with a snack."

All was quiet in the jungle.
Quiet as the trees growing towards the sky.
Quiet as the leaves reaching towards the light.
Quiet as a baby sleeping. Suddenly . . .

Chuckling
and chortling,

sniggering
and snickering.

The hyena was laughing.
Laughing like hyenas do.

But nobody knew what was so funny.

"Quiet!" said Pa Lion, as loud as he dared.
"It's all right," said Ma Lion. "Leo's still asleep."
"I can't eat the hyena, then," said Pa Lion crossly.
"No, my dear," said Ma Lion. "You can't eat the hyena."
"Bother!" said Pa Lion. "I'm beginning to feel quite peckish."

All was quiet in the jungle.
Quiet as the calm after a storm.
Quiet as sunshine after rain.
Quiet as a baby sleeping. Suddenly . . .

Howling and hooting, screeching and chattering.
Swinging and swooping. A family of monkeys was
leaping through the trees!

"Quiet!" said Pa Lion, as loud as he dared.
"It's all right," said Ma Lion. "Leo's still asleep."
"I can't eat the monkeys, then," said Pa Lion grumpily.
"No, my dear," said Ma Lion. "You can't eat the monkeys."
"Bother!" said Pa Lion. "I'm hungry now, really hungry."

It was the middle of the day
and the jungle was hot and humid.
The animals sheltered in the shade of the
trees, drowsy and dozing.

All was quiet in the jungle.
Quiet as the blazing sun.
Quiet as the shadows underneath the trees.
Quiet as a baby sleeping. Suddenly . . .

Splashing and squelching.

Ooohing and aaahing.

A hippopotamus was
yawning in the cool muddy
shallows of the river.

"**Quiet!**" said Pa Lion, as loud as he dared.
"It's all right," said Ma Lion. "Leo's still fast asleep."
"I can't eat the hippopotamus, then," said Pa Lion despairingly.
"Sometimes, my dear," said Ma Lion, "your eyes are bigger
than your belly. No, you can't eat the hippopotamus."
"Bother," said Pa Lion.

"I know this is wicked," thought Pa Lion,
rubbing his tummy, "but I do so wish someone would
make a little more noise, and wake up baby Leo.
Just for a minute."

But all was quiet in the jungle.
Quiet as a fish swimming in the river.
Quiet as a bird soaring in the sky.
Quiet as a baby sleeping. Suddenly . . .

A rumbling and grumbling,
a groaning and moaning,

a gurgling
and burbling.

A noise like nothing ever heard before.
Loud as thunder. Loud as banging drums.
Loud as a baby crying!

"Who has woken baby Leo?" cried Ma Lion.
"Find who it is, Pa. Find them and
eat them! Now!"

"It's me," said Pa Lion.
"It's my stomach rumbling.
I'm so hungry!"

Time to Sleep, Alfie Bear!

Catherine Walters

"It's nearly bedtime, Alfie," called
Mother Bear. She gathered up Alfie's baby
brother and sister, but Alfie didn't move.
    "It can't be bedtime," he complained.
"It's still light."
    "It's always light at bedtime in the
summer," said Mother Bear. "Come
along, Alfie, time for your bath."

123

Mother Bear took Alfie and
the babies to the lake.
   "We'll all have a nice relaxing bath
to make us sleepy," said Mother Bear.

Alfie sat by the water's edge. It was
still warm after a long sunny day and
the fish leapt to catch the evening flies.
   "Huh! The fish aren't going to bed,"
thought Alfie. "Why should I?"
   It gave him an idea . . .

"Look, Mother Bear," shouted Alfie.
"I don't have to go to bed! I'm a fish!"

He began to jump and dive and splash.
The babies loved it. They laughed and
splashed too.
    "Don't do that," sighed Mother Bear.
"The babies are getting too excited.
They'll never go to sleep."

When they had all calmed down,
Mother Bear took them back to
the cave.

"It's a warm night," she said.
"Go and get some nice, cool
grass for bedding, Alfie. That
will help you sleep."

Alfie went outside and pulled
up a few pawfuls of grass.

Over in the meadow, some owls were
swooping, ready for their evening hunt.
  "The owls aren't going to bed,"
thought Alfie. "Why should I?"

131

Alfie rushed back into the cave and began to flap his arms. Grass flew everywhere.

"Look! I'm an owl!" he hooted. "I don't need to go to bed. I'm just getting up!"

"Oh Alfie, stop that!" groaned Mother Bear. "Look, the babies are throwing all their lovely bedding around, too. None of you will have anywhere to sleep."

At last, Alfie and the babies were safely
in bed but still they didn't go to sleep.
"I think you need a nice, gentle song,"
said Mother Bear. "Now, close your eyes."
Alfie wasn't listening. Outside, he
could hear wolves howling.
"The wolves aren't going to sleep,"
he thought. "Why should I?"

"Look, I'm a wolf! AAAAOOOW!" said Alfie.

"OW, OW, OW!" shrieked the babies, kicking their feet.

Mother Bear wasn't pleased. "That's enough, Alfie," she growled. "I don't want any little wolves in the cave. You can wait outside until the babies are asleep."

"Hooray!" cried Alfie, running outside.
The sun had set and the air was full
of dust and shadows. Alfie charged
across the meadow, tipped back his
head, and howled again,
"AAAAOOOW!"
Then, from somewhere close by,
someone answered him,
"AAAAOOOW!"

Alfie jumped. There in front of him was
a wolf cub, with his family close by.

The cub sniffed him all over.

"Are you a wolf?" it asked. "You sound
like one, but you don't look like one."

"All little wolf cubs should be in bed
by now," growled Mother Wolf.

"Are you sure you're a wolf?" called
a big, gruff voice . . .

"... because you look like a little bear to me!"
It was Father Bear, coming to take
him home.
"I'm a bear, I'm a bear!" shouted Alfie.
The big wolves turned and walked away.
"Goodnight, little bear," called the
wolf cub, following them into the trees.

Father Bear snuggled Alfie into his fur.

"So you're a bear?" he said. "But are you a sleepy bear all ready for bed?"

Night had fallen, and the sky sparkled with stars.

"No," said Alfie. "I'm not –"

But before he could finish speaking, he had fallen fast asleep.

Two Hungry Bears

Linda Cornwell and Jane Chapman

Big Brown Bear and
Little Bear shared a
cosy cave. They shared
each other's company . . .

150

and they shared
each other's food.
Little Bear nibbled
round the edges . . .

152

and Big Brown Bear
munched up the middles.
In this way, they got
along very well.

But one very bright autumn day, Little Bear woke up feeling EXTRA hungry and Big Brown Bear woke up feeling MONSTROUSLY hungry!

"I'll buy some food for both of us," said Little Bear.

"That's very kind of you, Little Bear," answered Big Brown Bear sleepily, and he crept right back to bed.

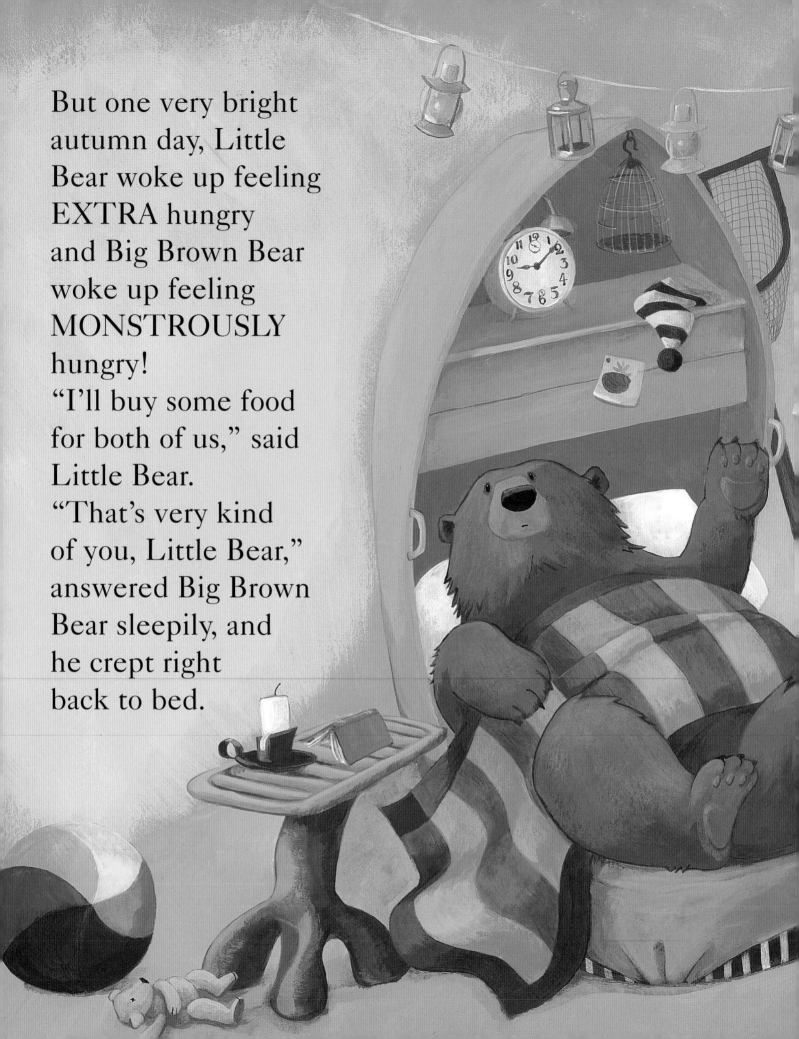

Little Bear went out
shopping and bought
some things to take
back to Big Brown
Bear. But she found
she was so hungry . . .

that she ate everything
straight away –
pies and pastries,
peanuts and puddings,

chocolates and cheeses,
crisps and cakes –

from sides to middles,
middles to sides
AND BACK AGAIN!

Meanwhile, Big Brown Bear's tummy was
RRRRUMMMBLING rather loudly – so loudly
that the walls of the cave began to shake.
"I've been thinking," said Big Brown Bear,
"perhaps *I* should be out shopping for Little Bear."
So off he went with his big bag . . .

159

but when he had filled
it right up, he was so
hungry that he found
he could not wait.

He began by
munching just
the middles.

But then he set to work on sausages,
strawberries and sandwiches,
not to mention tangerines,
toffee apples and treacle tarts . . .

AND
hamburgers,
custard and
chips . . .

AND
biscuits,
spaghetti
and soup . . .

AND
pizzas, salads and
ice-creams . . .

AND
tomatoes,
jellies and
corn on the cob –
and one small
grape.

Big Brown Bear ate tops, bottoms,
sides and middles.
There was just no stopping him!

But when he had finished eating,
he began to feel very, very full
and very, very guilty.
He had left nothing for Little Bear.

Big Brown Bear staggered back home where
Little Bear was waiting patiently for him.
"Did you find any nice middles to munch?"
Little Bear asked him.
"*I can see that you did!*" she thought to herself.
Big Brown Bear could only nod his head.

"Did you come across any tasty edges to nibble?"
asked Big Brown Bear.
"*It certainly looks as though you might have!*"
he thought to himself.

168

They sat
down together –
rather carefully.
"I saved you half
of a cream cracker,"
said Big Brown Bear.
"It still has four
edges to nibble."
"I saved you three
quarters of a banana,"
said Little Bear.
"It's all middle –
no edges
at all!"

After a while, Big Brown Bear yawned. "I think I'll skip supper," he said. "I'm feeling a little too tired." "An early night will do us both good," agreed Little Bear. They spent an awfully long time brushing their teeth . . .

before Big Brown Bear snuggled into his
bed, and Little Bear crept quietly into hers.
"Let's collect the food together tomorrow,"
yawned Big Brown Bear.
But tomorrow was a long, long time away
because . . .

Big Brown Bear and
Little Bear slept, with
their tummies nicely full,
all through the winter until
SPRING!

172

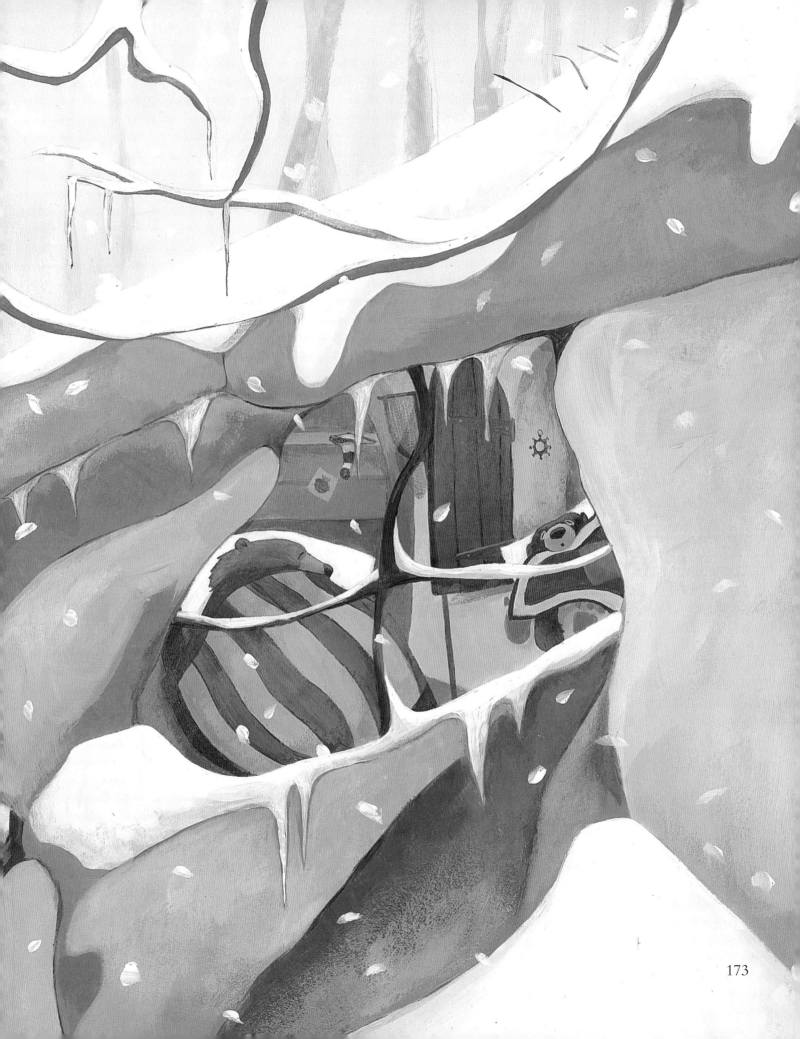